RAWR!

By Todd H. Doodler

Scholastic Press • New York

To my daughter Elle, who taught
me how to RAWR with joy!
— T.D.

Library of Congress Cataloging-in-Publication Data is available.

ISBN 978-0-545-51118-6   ISBN 9781407139524 (UK)

10 9 8 7 6 5 4 3 2 1   13 14 15 16 17

Printed in China 95   First printing, September 2013

Design by Pamela Notarantonio

New Material Only   Matériaux neufs seulement
Reg. No. 04T-00218610   No de permis 04T-00218610
Content: Polyurethane Foam   Contenu: Mousse de polyuréthane

Being a dinosaur is hard.

I am bigger
than every kid
in my class.

I am bigger than my teachers, too.

I am even bigger than the school bus.

My desk does not fit.

My gym clothes do not fit.

And I am not very good
at hide-and-seek.

Because I am big, some people think I am scary.

But they are wrong.

I am helpful.

I have good table manners.

And my smile is really something.

So what are people afraid of?

Here is a little secret:

means **HELLO** in Dinosaur!
Please tell all your friends.

And being BIG can be a good thing.

I am very good
at sports.

I can find things when they get lost.

And I can be a lot of fun at recess.

So if you meet a dinosaur,

RAAAAWW